The SCARIEST KITTEN in the World

by Terrifying Kitten

(with help from **KATE MESSNER**)

illustrated by **MACKENZIE HALEY**

Farrar Straus Giroux
New York

WARNING
THIS IS A VERY SCARY STORY.
IT'S SO CREEPY AND SPINE-TINGLING THAT IT WILL SCARE YOU
RIGHT OUT OF YOUR SNEAKERS.
ARE YOU SURE YOU WANT TO READ THIS STORY?
YOU COULD FIND YOURSELF A BOOK ABOUT RAINBOWS
OR FRIENDLY UNICORNS INSTEAD.
NO?
ALL RIGHT, THEN. YOU ASKED FOR IT.

For my favorite felines:
Mama, Batman, Fergus, Milo, Eddie the Smacker, Boudleaux,
Addie, Beezus, Percy, Hazel, Petra, Barnaby, and Hex
—K.M.

For Arwen, the first kitty in my life. You gave me unconditional,
consistent love when I needed it the most. Sixteen years passed
in the blink of an eye. I'll always love you baby girl.
—M.H.

Farrar Straus Giroux Books for Young Readers
An imprint of Macmillan Publishing Group, LLC
120 Broadway, New York, NY 10271 • mackids.com

Library of Congress Control Number: 2022949539

First edition, 2023
Color separations by Bright Arts (H.K.) Ltd.
Printed in China by RR Donnelley Asia Printing Solutions Ltd.,
Dongguan City, Guangdong Province

ISBN 978-0-374-39005-1
1 3 5 7 9 10 8 6 4 2

The art in this book was created using good old fashioned pencil and paper, then digitally
painted in Photoshop. The text was set in Cosmiqua, and the display type was Garamouche.
Designed and art directed by Sharismar Rodriguez. Production was supervised by Allene Cassagnol,
and the production editor was Kat Kopit. Edited by Janine O'Malley.

Once upon a time, on a dark and stormy night, some kids JUST LIKE YOU found a TERRIFYING HAUNTED HOUSE.

At the end of a long hallway was a ragged old door—all splintery and creaky.

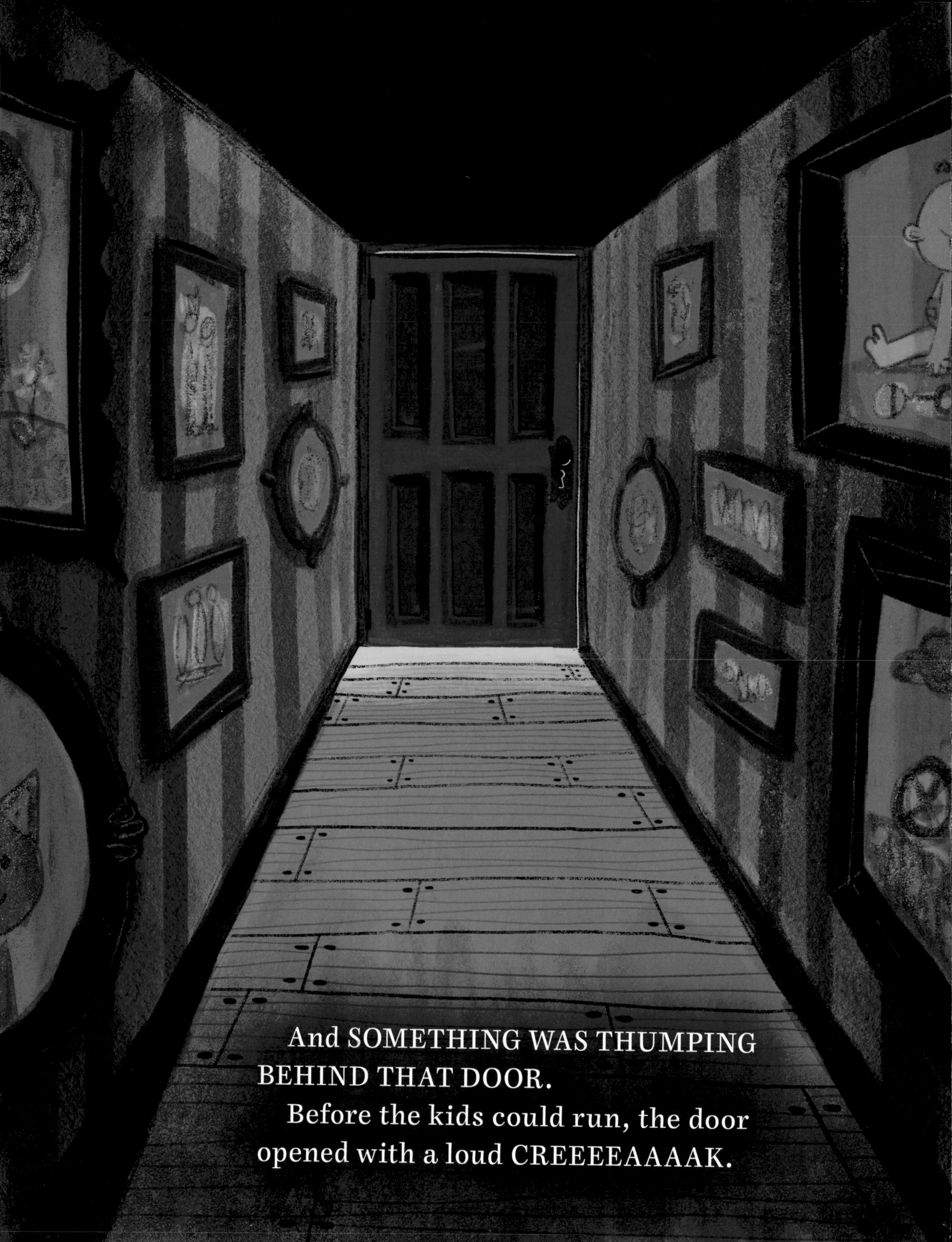

And SOMETHING WAS THUMPING BEHIND THAT DOOR.

Before the kids could run, the door opened with a loud CREEEEAAAAK.

Lightning flashed, and a menacing shadow darkened the floor. It was the fiercest, most horrifying creature the kids had ever seen. Suddenly, it opened its gaping mouth, and . . .

Are you sure you want to turn the page? Seeing this ferocious monster and hearing its bone-chilling growl could FREEZE YOUR LITTLE HEART TO ICE.

It’s not too late for you to choose a different book about something more pleasant. Like ice cream sandwiches or new crayons or picking flowers in the sunshine.

You're still here? Fine. When you turn the page and have to run screaming for your mama, don't say I didn't warn you.

Okay, then . . . The creature opened its gaping mouth and let out a bone-chilling roar.

Grrrrarrrr!

Hey, quit laughing . . .
Can’t you see how scary this is?
Hold on . . .

SNARL!
GROWL!
ROARRRRRRR!

Hmm. You don't look scared. But I bet deep inside, you are shaking in your sneakers. You're just *pretending* to be one of those kids who's not afraid of anything.

DO NOT MAKE ME CALL MY TERRIFYING FRIENDS.

Fine.

NOW YOU'RE IN BIG TROUBLE. TURN ONE MORE PAGE, AND YOU'LL GET THE SCARE OF YOUR LIFE.

You turned the page! What were you thinking?!

Trust me, you REALLY don't want to turn another one.

You're going to do it again, aren't you?

Woof.

No!

No!

No!

Come back when you can be TERRIFYING.

Can somebody please show these two how it's done?

Boo!

I said
BOOOOO!!

Rats. I don't think
I scared them either.

Don't worry—I've got this. If they turn the page again, they are going to be SO STINKING SCARED!

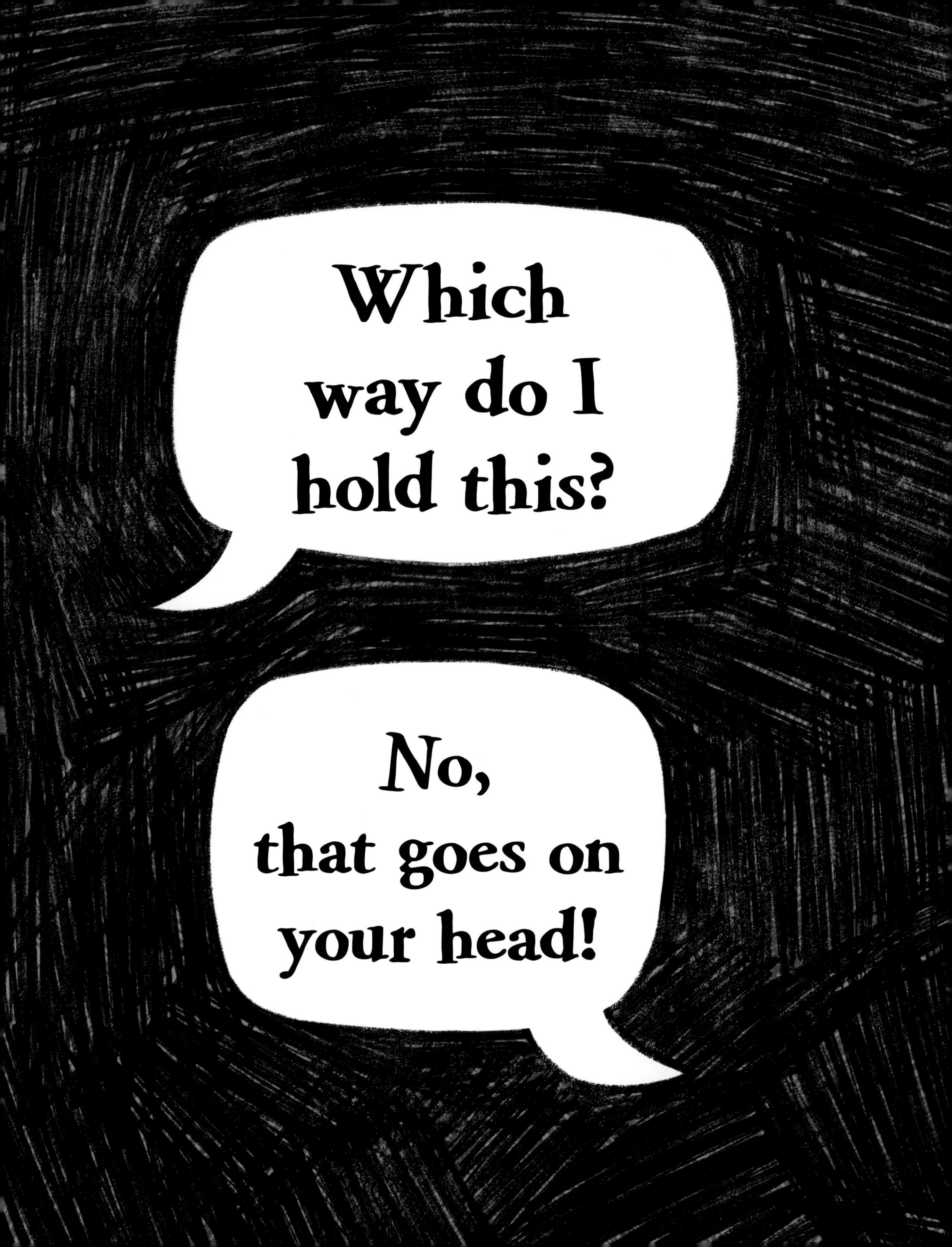

Which
way do I
hold this?

No,
that goes on
your head!

This is making my ears itch.

Just put it on!

Okay, we're ready!

BEHOLD TH

very big scary red panda
ghost of a Bloodthirsty duckling
WoOoOoOoOo!
WoOoOoOo!
Grrrr!
Must. Eat. Brains . . .
scary zombie sloth

HE TERROR!

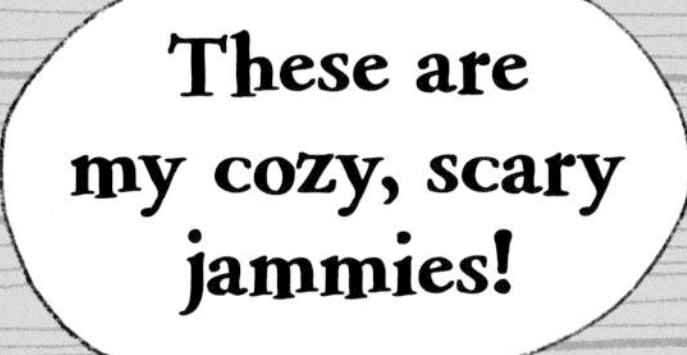

Spooky baby goat

Vampire puppy

I vant to drink your bloooooood!

DaNGErously prickly HEdgehog

Hissssss!!

Did it work?
Were they scared?
I don't think so.
Ghost of a Bloodthirsty duckling
scary zombie sloth

THUMP!
THUMP!
THUMP!
Vampire puppy
Spooky baby goat

“Bath time!”

And then, in the glowing light of the full moon, the very scary creatures had a bath and went to bed.